EMERGENCY MONSTER SQUAD

BY DAVE HOROWITZ

NANCY PAULSEN BOOKS

WEEEE WOOOO WE

For all the medics and EMTs working tonight.

NANCY PAULSEN BOOKS
An imprint of Penguin Random House LLC, New York

Visit us online at penguinrandomhouse.com

Library of Congress Cataloging-in-Publication Data
Names: Horowitz, Dave, 1970- author, illustrator. | Title: Emergency Monster Squad / Dave Horowitz.
Description: New York: Nancy Paulsen Books, [2020] | Summary: "EMS workers driving an 'amboolance' come to the aid of injured monsters"–Provided by publisher. | Identifiers: LCCN 2019037090 | ISBN 9780399548505 (hardcover) | ISBN 9780399548512 (ebk) | ISBN 9780399548536 (kindle edition)
Subjects: CYAC: Stories in rhyme. | Ambulances–Fiction. | Monsters–Fiction.
Classification: LCC PZ8.3.H7848 Em 2020 | DDC [E]–dc23
LC record available at https://lccn.loc.gov/2019037090

Manufactured in China by RR Donnelley Asia Printing Solutions Ltd.
ISBN 9780399548505
1 3 5 7 9 10 8 6 4 2

Design by Nicole Rheingans | Text set in KG Blank Space and KG Behind These Hazel Eyes
The art was done with construction paper, charcoal, and colored pencils.

Everyone knows who the police are.
Everyone knows what firefighters do.
But do you know what EMS is?

EMS stands for **Emergency Medical Services**, the people you call when someone gets very sick or injured. When you call **911** and ask for help, EMS shows up in an ambulance. They've got all the equipment and know-how to patch up a wound, help someone who is ill, and sometimes even restart a stopped heart.

No matter where you are or what time of day it is, EMS is always there and ready to help. But don't call **911** unless it's really an emergency. (And please, whatever you do, don't say the "q-word.")

PARAMEDIC
EMT
MEDIC
EMT
EMT
LUNCH BOX
EMT (EMERGENCY MEDICAL TECHNICIAN)

This is Sally,
and this is Gus—
two heroes who ride
on the Monster Squad bus.

It's a difficult thing,
to be called to save lives.
So Sally gets ready.
Gus mostly drives.

PORTABLE OXYGEN TANK

CARDIAC MONITOR
AND DEFIBRILLATOR

MEDI

CHECK LIST
Monitor
Med Bag
Oxygen
Coffee
Snacks

EMT
HAT
EMT
FIRST-IN BAG
(medical stuff)

Slurp
AMBOOLANCE
A BUG

There's only one thing,
and we swear this is true:
Please don't say "QUIET"
'round an ambulance crew.

'Cause once you say "QUIET,"
ya know what comes next?

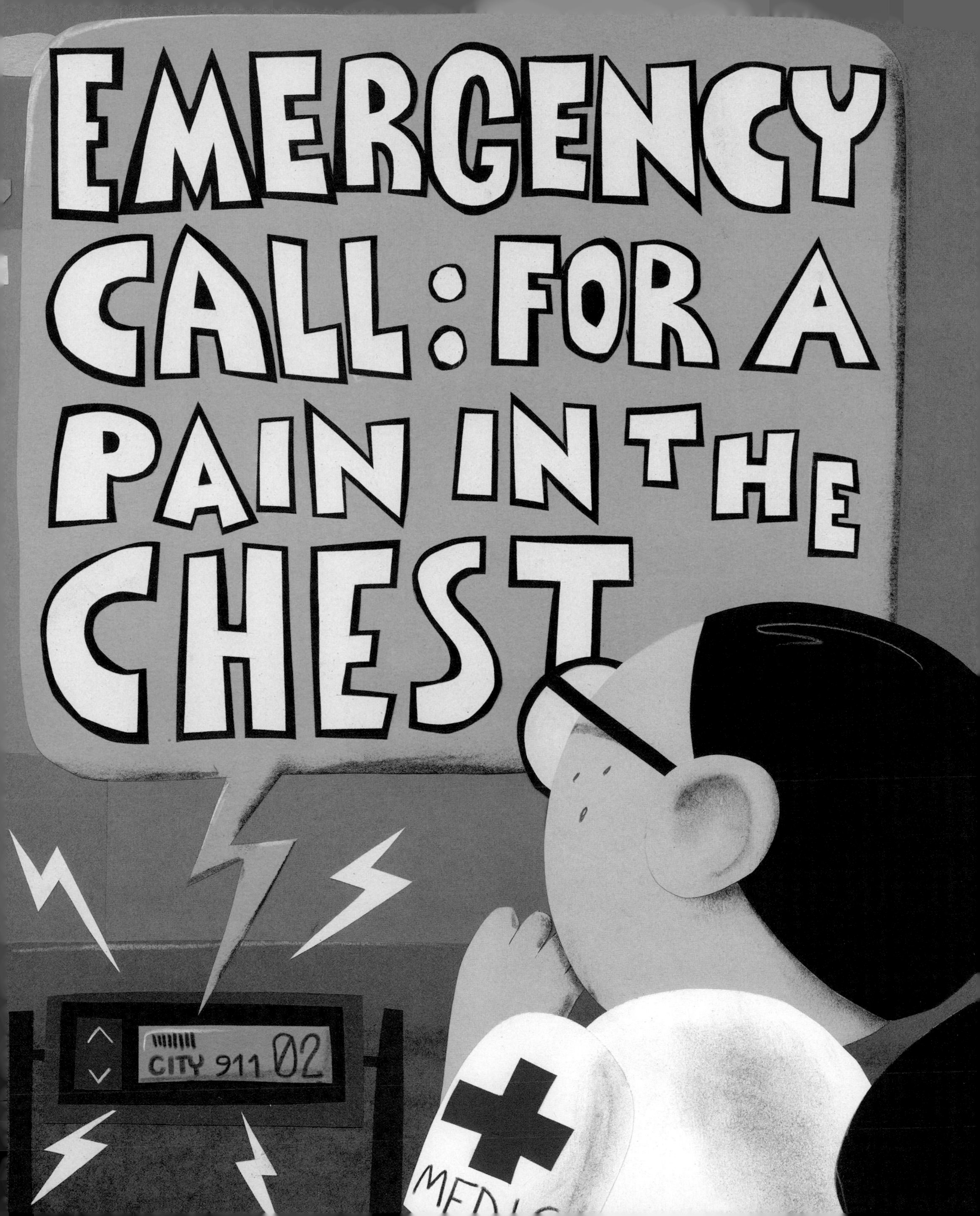
EMERGENCY CALL: FOR A PAIN IN THE CHEST
CITY 911 02

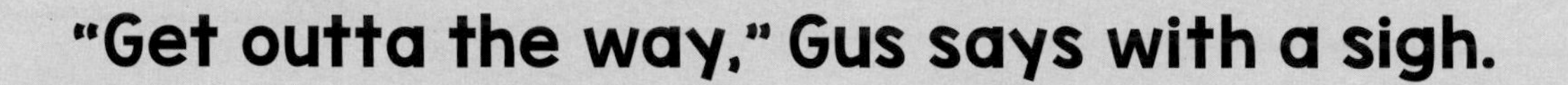

"Get outta the way," Gus says with a sigh.

And everyone does, except for one guy.

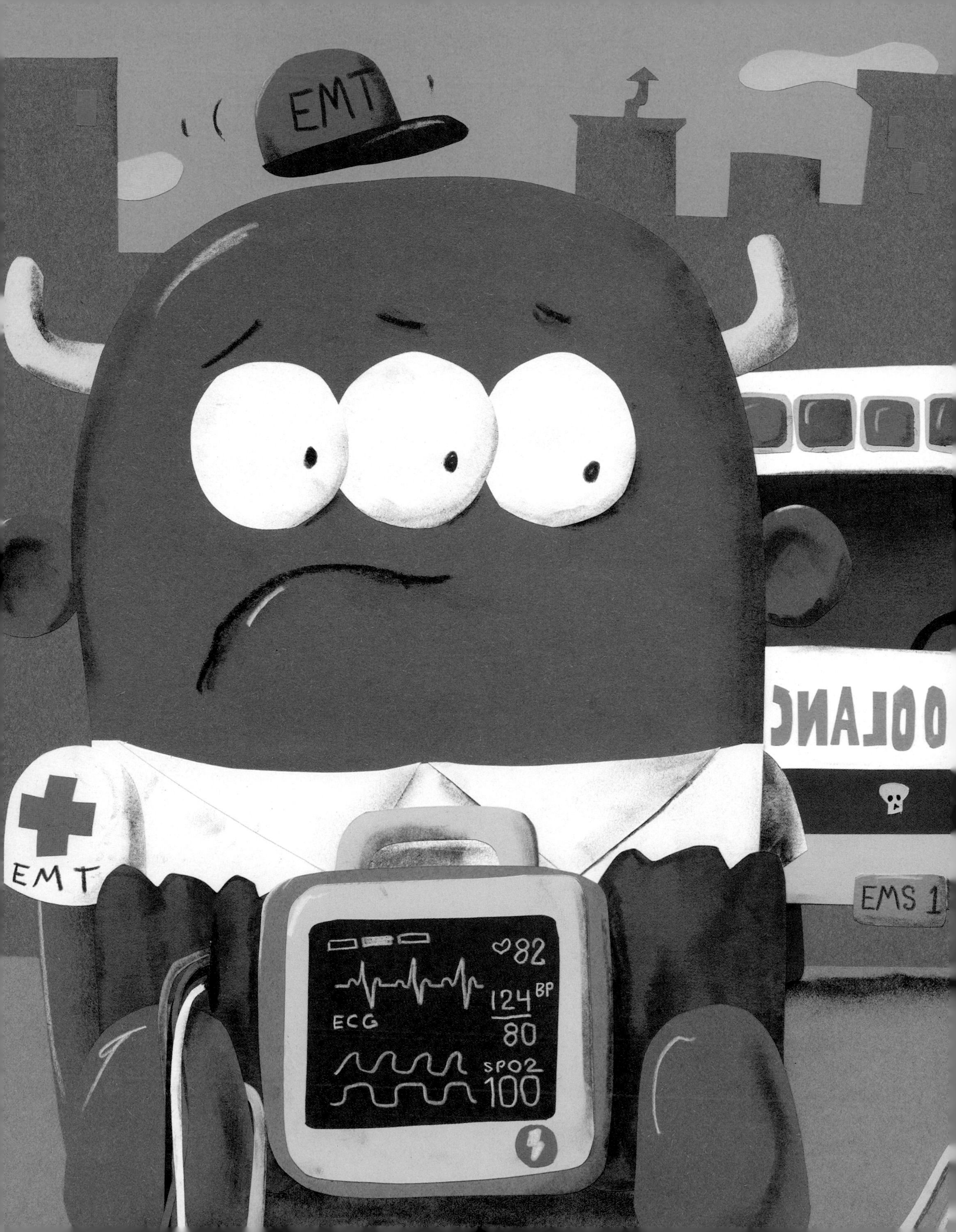
EMT
EMT
EMS 1
82
ECG
124 BP
80
SPO2
100

At last on the scene,
there's a zombie called Bill.
He's sweating profusely
and says he feels ill.

Sally runs a few tests,
as a good medic should,
and everything's normal,
which, for a zombie, ain't good.

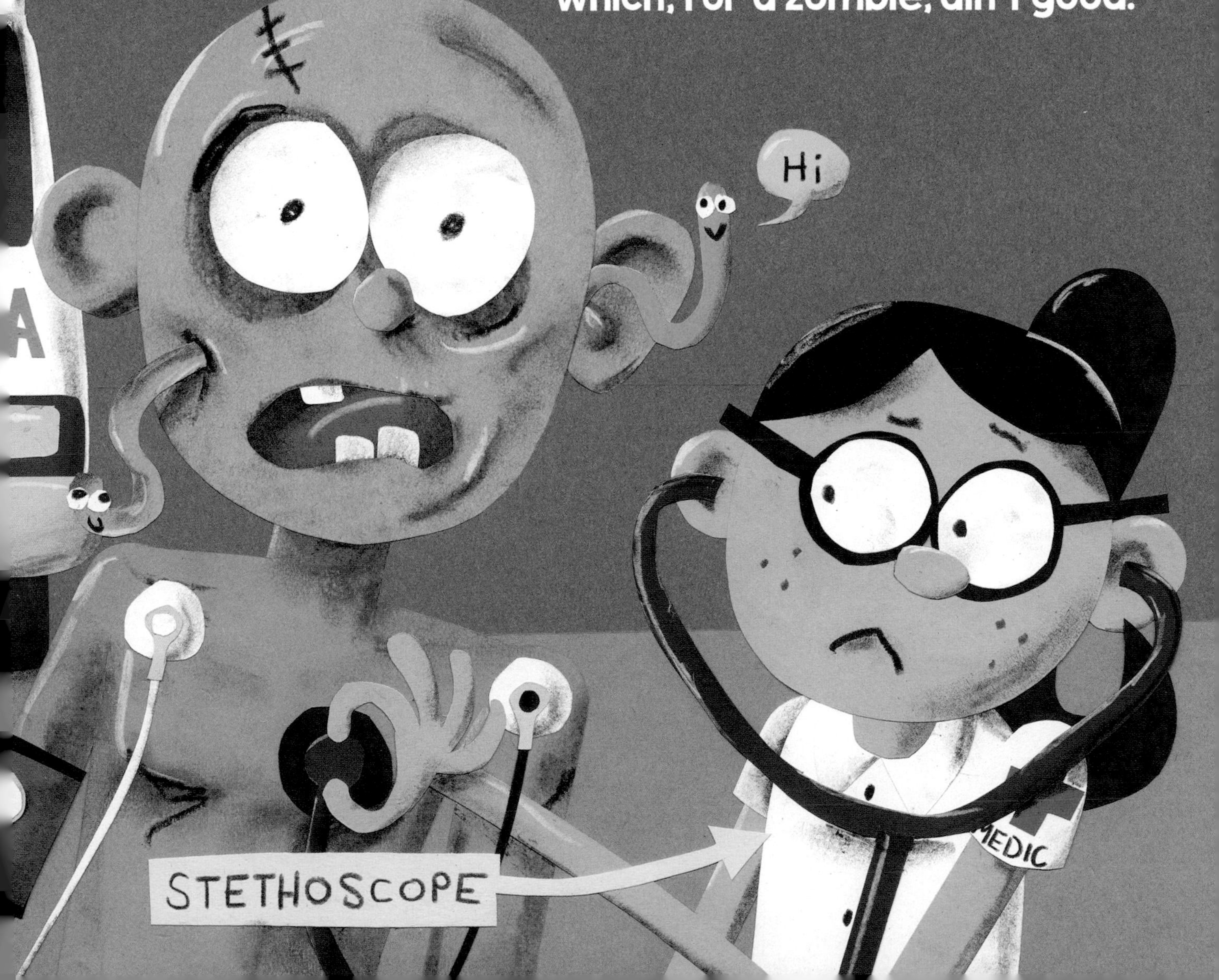

WEE WOO

So it's off to the hospital,
fast as they can.
Gus turns on the lights
and the sirens, and then . . .

!!!

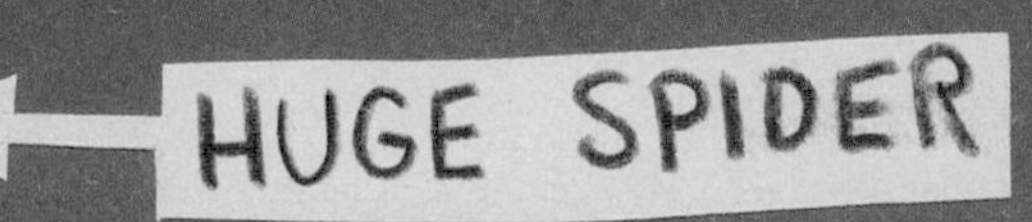

CAT?
AMBOOLANCE
AMBOOLANCE
EMS 1

500 mL
IV BAG
MEDIC
EMS 1
BIKE PARTS

"LOOK OUT!" There's a
skeleton down in the street.
He seems to be missing
the bones in his feet.

His kneecap is off
and so is one shin.
Gus pulls the truck over.
Sally tells him, "Hop in."

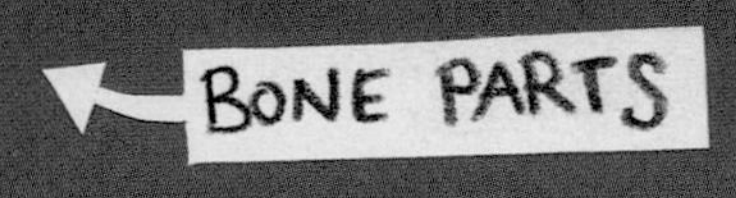

"Ugh!" says the zombie.
"I have a request.
Can you all just be QUIET?
I'm trying to rest!"

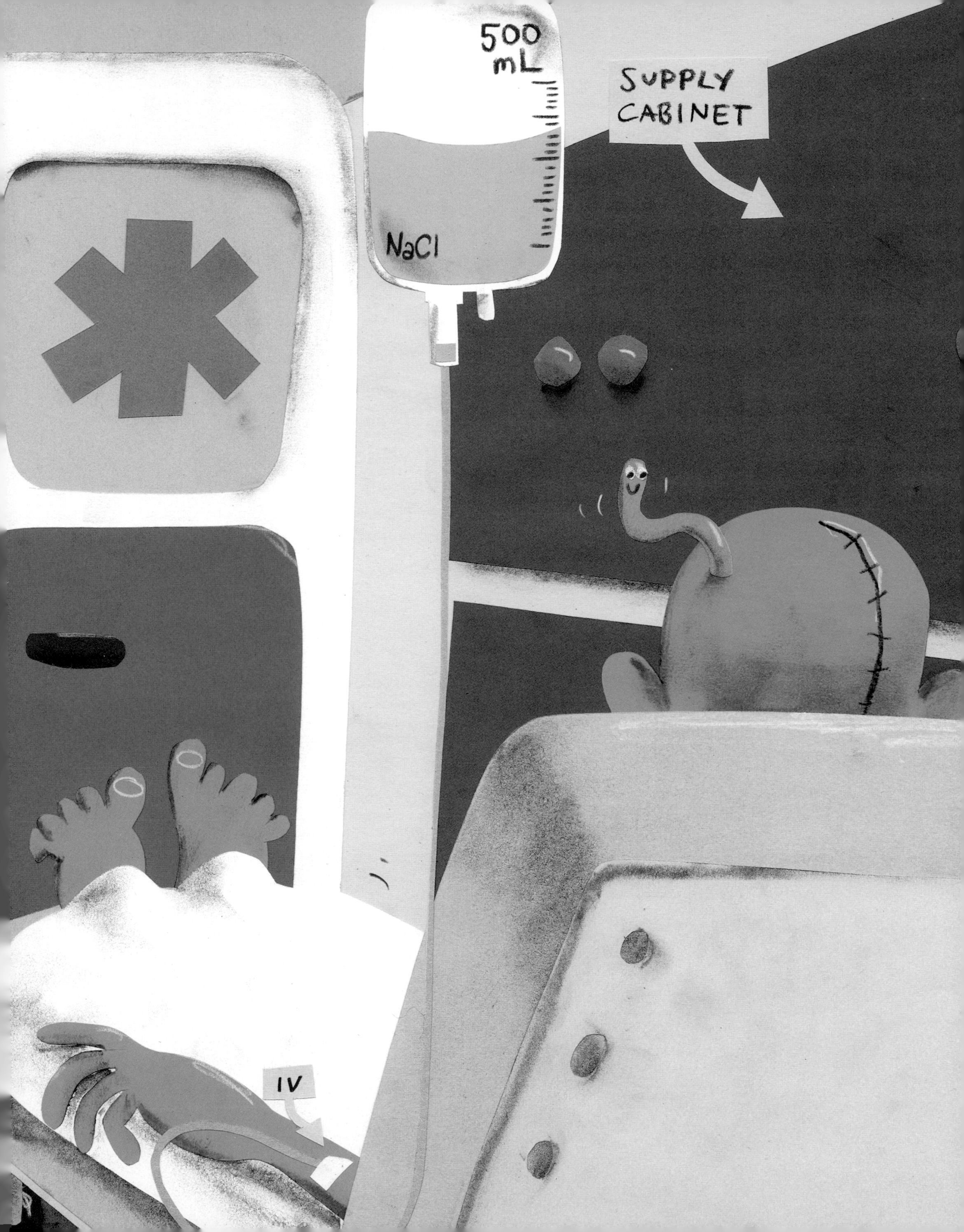
500 mL
NaCl
SUPPLY CABINET
IV

Did someone say "QUIET"?
Did that really just happen?
Then outta the shadows
comes Ol' Mama Kraken.

Yes, Ol' Mama Kraken
is in need of a hand.
Her eggs are all hatching,
and she's stuck on dry land.

HALP!

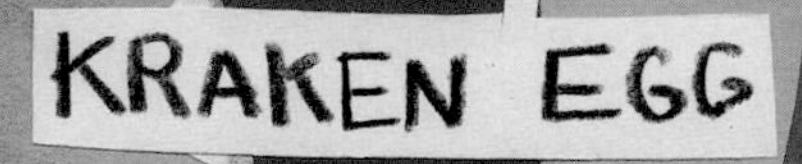
KRAKEN EGG

CRACKIN' EGG

CRACKIN' EGG

MEDIC

Gus pulls the truck over
and she climbs in the back.
And soon as she does,
the eggs start to CRACK!

WEE
THAT GUY
(AGAIN)

WOO

And again they get rolling—
to the hospital, quick—
with the newborns, the
injured, and also the sick.

At last, all good monsters
arrive, safe and sound.
They together say, "Thank you,"
and then something profound:

Thanks,
bruh.

EMERGE
Thank you!
MEDIC
STRETCHER

YOU GUYS ARE OUR

HEROES.

YOU'RE REALLY THE BEST . . .

HOPE THE REST OF YOUR NIGHT'S

QUIET

AND Y'ALL GET SOME REST.

Help!
Unit 1?
EMT
AMBOOLANCE

GLOSSARY

AMBULANCE (aka **THE BUS**): a truck with flashy lights and sirens that takes the sick and injured to the hospital

BANDAGE: cloth that wraps around a wound and keeps it clean

BIKE PARTS: the parts of a bike

BONE PARTS: the parts of a skeleton

BUG: any creepy-crawly with six, eight, or a million legs

CARDIAC MONITOR & DEFIBRILLATOR: a high-tech portable device that can monitor a heart rhythm, check vitals, and even deliver a shock to restart a stopped heart—serious business!

CAT?: a cat that may not be a cat—I mean, we are in Monster Town

CRACKIN' EGG (see also **KRAKEN EGG**): an egg that is hatching

EMT

EMT: Emergency Medical Technician; a person trained in basic life support

FEMUR: the upper leg bone, the largest bone in the human body

FEMUR

FIBULA: the smaller of the two lower leg bones, the one that isn't the tibia

FIRST-IN BAG: the bag that an EMT or medic carries onto a scene that holds everything they may need for the emergency

HAT: come on, you know what a hat is

HUGE SPIDER: a spider that happens to be huge

IV: a needle used to gain access to the bloodstream (Yikes!); IV stands for "intravenous" (into the vein)

IV BAG (see also **IV**): a bag of fluid that is connected to an IV

KRAKEN EGG (see also **CRACKIN' EGG**): the unhatched egg of a kraken

PARAMEDIC: a person trained in advanced life support

PARAMEDIC

PATELLA: the kneecap

PORTABLE OXYGEN TANK: a tank full of oxygen to help people who are having trouble breathing

QUIET: the word we just don't say (I mean, unless you're trying to jinx us.)

RADIO: a two-way communication device that tells the ambulance crew where to go

STETHOSCOPE: a device used to listen to the heart and lungs

STRETCHER (aka **COT** or **GURNEY**): a bed with wheels

SUPPLY CABINET: where all the other stuff is

THAT GUY: that one guy, the one you don't want to be like

TIBIA: the bigger of the two lower leg bones, aka the shin bone